GRANDPA MUDCAKE and the Crazy Tea Party

Written and Illustrated
by Sophia J. Ferguson

For Max

First published in Great Britain 2021 by Macnaughtan Books
Text and illustration copyright © Sophia J. Ferguson

ISBN: 978-1-914523-04-5

This is Grandpa Mudcake.

Today he's sitting in the sunshine in his garden.

A lady called Sheena has moved into the house next door.

Sheena has been singing in her garden all day.

Grandpa is NOT enjoying the noise.

In fact, he's starting to get a bit grumpy.

Suddenly, Sheena appears over the garden fence.

"Hiya!" she calls to Grandpa, "My name's Sheena and I like chatting and shopping."

"What do you like?" she asks Grandpa.

Grandpa does NOT like chatting or shopping.

He doesn't want to talk to Sheena.

He quickly rushes indoors without saying hello.

The next day, Grandpa is sitting in his garden again.
A large cat jumps onto the garden fence.
"That must be Sheena's cat" Grandpa thinks
to himself.
Grandpa doesn't like cats.
"Get off the fence!" he shouts angrily at the cat.
But the cat just sits and stares at him.

Sheena pops her head over the fence again.

"This is my cat, Derek" she says to Grandpa.

"Do NOT lean or sit on the fence" shouts Grandpa, "It's wobbly!"

But Sheena and Derek don't listen to Grandpa. Each day, the fence gets more and more wobbly, and Grandpa gets more and more grumpy.

One day, Grandpa is asleep in his garden when he's woken by an enormous CRASH.
The garden fence has collapsed!
Sheena is lying on her back in Grandpa's garden.
There are bits of broken fence all over the grass.
"Sorry Mr Mudcake, I'll get it fixed" shouts Sheena.
Grandpa is VERY VERY angry.

Well, Sheena eventually had the garden fence fixed.
She's been very quiet for the last few weeks.
Grandpa is feeling much happier.
Today, he's enjoying the sunshine again in his garden.
Soon, he's fast asleep.
But he's not asleep for long.

Grandpa is woken by something tickling his nose.
It's Derek's tail.
"Go away!" Grandpa shouts at Derek.
To make things worse, Sheena is now playing loud pop music in her garden.
Oh dear, poor Grandpa.

"Turn that music off!" Grandpa shouts over the fence.

But Sheena can't hear him.

She's too busy singing and dancing in her garden.

Grandpa fetches a ladder.

He climbs up the ladder and peers over the fence.

In Sheena's garden he sees something amazing.

In the middle of Sheena's garden is a round table.
On the table is a huge mountain of cakes
and buns.
Grandpa can't believe his eyes.
There are cupcakes, cream buns, chocolate eclairs,
doughnuts and two large chocolate cakes.
Grandpa's mouth is watering.

"I'm having a crazy tea party!" says Sheena.
"Come and get some cakes before all my friends
arrive" she says to Grandpa.
Grandpa is quiet for a moment.
He loves cakes.
"That's very kind. I'll come straight over"
he replies.

Grandpa quickly rushes round to Sheena's house.

Sheena hands him a large tray.

"Take as many cakes as you like!" she laughs.

Grandpa can't believe his luck.

He piles lots of cakes and buns onto the tray.

"Thank you Sheena. I do hope you enjoy your crazy tea party" he says, politely.

Grandpa heads home with his tray.
Soon, there's lots of VERY loud music and
singing coming from Sheena's garden.
But Grandpa's enjoying his cakes so much
that he hardly notices the terrible noise.
He doesn't even notice Derek who's joined
him to escape the party.

Here's Grandma Mudcake.

She's just arrived home from her shopping trip.

"Where did you get those cakes?" she asks
Grandpa.

"And what's that TERRIBLE noise?" she gasps.

"Sheena's having a crazy tea party" he explains.

"Sheena's my new friend" he adds.

Grandma is VERY surprised to hear all of this.

Well, Sheena now has her tea party every Friday.
And Grandpa always gets his cakes beforehand.
He's bought some special headphones to block out Sheena's noisy music.
Friday is Grandpa's favourite day of the week.
He's even made friends with Derek.
"Sheena's crazy but I like her" Grandpa chuckles to himself.

Books by Sophia J. Ferguson:

For fun stuff, visit:
www.reginald-stinkbottom.com

CPSIA information can be obtained
at www.ICGtesting.com
Printed in the USA
LVHW070915260122
709436LV00001B/20